Journey of My Aneurysm

LaShaya Porter Miller

Journey of My Aneurysm

ISBN: 978-1-964283-65-4

Dedication

Journey of My Aneurysm is dedicated to my Village, which is my family, my church family, my physical therapists, St. Mary's Hospital ICU staff, Dr. Stofko, and all those who have played a vital role in my healing process. Thank you, I love you all.

Acknowledgment

"Mommy, wake up," was what Zane said to me. Thank you, Zane, for being my son, pushing me to be great, always rooting me on, and protecting me when I was being made fun of. Not being ashamed of me for being in a wheelchair at times or using a cane. You've hugged me when I've cried, you've looked after my feelings when you thought I was lonely, and you've always made sure I was ok, even at a young age. You've been the reason I go so hard. You are the reason why I didn't give up. You definitely live up to the meaning of your name, God's gracious gift. This is for you. Thank you, son. I love you to infinity.

Love,

Mom

Table of Contents

Chapter 1 – Introduction

Picture Taken a Month Before Aneurysm

My name is LaShaya Porter Miller, and I am known as Shay. As a child, I was diagnosed with Sickle Cell Anemia at six months. My parents, Lewis, and Deborah Porter, have always taken excellent care of me; being that my disease kept me in and out of the hospital due to sickle cell crises, the Lord always showed his mercy and grace, allowing me to get to school. The illness was hard at times; the sickle cell crisis came out of the blue due to stress, anxiety, and getting too cold. If it was a severe crisis, I could have been hospitalized for several days.

I attended a small Christian school, Knoxville Baptist Christian School, and graduated in May 1999. I accepted Jesus Christ as my Lord and Savior at a young age. I'm very close to my family. I grew up close to my cousins; we are like sisters and brothers. I attended Carson Newman College right after high school, now known as Carson Newman University. I was able to contain any major sickle cell pain with a medication, hydroxyurea, which I started taking right before my freshman year at Carson Newman. I graduated with a bachelor's in Computer Information Systems in July 2003. Then, I went on to work at a couple of banks as an Executive Administrative Assistant. in Business Banking. I married Sanford Miller, Jr., in September 2008. I have a stepson, Tyson Ray Miller, whom I met when he was three years old, and my Zane Ray Miller, who is now eleven years old.

Family – From Left to Right – Me, Zane Ray Miller, Tyson Ray Miller, Sanford Miller, Jr.

Picture taken Christmas Eve, 2016

Picture taken Christmas Morning before aneurysm.

Chapter 2 – Christmas Day 2016: The Fall

Christmas Eve 2016, after finishing last-minute shopping, decorating, and wrapping gifts. I went to bed with a major headache, thinking it was just due to stress and maybe sinuses, combined with being tired, so I took Excedrin, which I would normally take, because I was having mini headaches on and off, thought I would sleep it off and feel better.

The next morning, Christmas day, we got up, opened gifts, got dressed, and got ready for church. We had to pick Tyson up after church, which worked out for the better, not really knowing what would happen. I took time to put some gifts in a bag to take with us. Before I knew it, I was passed out on the steps of our apartment. I faintly remember a little voice saying, "Mommy, wake up." Sanford had no idea what happened. He called several family members, but at that time, no one answered. He then called Emergency 911. He was finally able to contact with his Mom. They came to us as quickly as they could. The ambulance went down the wrong street. Sanford panicked at that point and had to flag them down. I was foaming at the mouth. Emergency saw that I was completely out of it; they had to get me off the steps and cut off my shirt and jacket. Zane went with his grandparents. We were on our way to the hospital; the closest one was Tennova St Mary's, which was perfect because one of the top Neurosurgeons in the country was working on Christmas Day, which was nothing BUT GOD. If I had gone to another hospital, they would have sent me to

Dr. Stofko because he's one of the top Neurosurgeons in the country. He was the only doctor in the area who could perform the type of detailed surgery I needed. Praise the Lord that I got to the hospital when I did. If I had gotten there any later, I wouldn't have made it. I was wheeled into the ER. I was out of it, but my Mom told me I was pointing to the right side of my head. I was rushed back quickly and had a CT scan and MRI. At that time, no one really knew what was wrong after the results. Sanford and my parents were told I had a ruptured brain aneurysm, formally called right anterior cerebral artery aneurysm, and bleeding on the brain. I also had six other aneurysms. and was bleeding on the brain. Dr. Stofko and his team coiled[1] the aneurysm. I also was given twenty-six units of blood in surgery.

After several hours of surgery, and once everything was complete, Dr. Stofko explained the extent of the surgery. I had what's formally called a decompressive hemicraniectomy, which means removing the right side of the skull in order for the swelling to go down and what could possibly be a side effect of the ruptured aneurysm. I was taken to recovery. My family was told that I may not walk or be able to move my left side. I was hooked on a couple of machines and a ventilator. My head also looked like a piece was missing out, but it was not exposed. The right side of my head was dented in; it was wrapped and bandaged up.

When anyone saw me, my parents told me they were confused about why my head looked like it did. Dr. Stofko

---

[1] Coiling: a procedure, performed during an angiogram, in which platinum coils are inserted into an aneurysm. < https://mayfieldclinic.com/pe-coiling.htm>

explained why my head was deformed. I was on a ventilator, and only my immediate family could see me. Sanford was right there and just held my hand. Several family, friends, and church members were in the ICU waiting room to pray and be there for Sanford and my parents. The one I call my big baby, Tyson, was thirteen years old at the time and came in to see me. My body was attached to many machines, and I hated that he had to see me in that state. He was heartbroken, but since no one didn't know what would happen to me, he could at least see me. It was like a big family reunion in the ICU waiting room without me, but because of me. They were there throughout the entire time that I was in surgery. Many brought food and drinks and had collective prayer with my family right there in the ICU waiting room. Those prayers brought me through. This could have happened in an entirely different way. I could have had the ruptured aneurysm in my sleep that Christmas Eve and no one would have known why I wasn't waking up. Instead, Jesus saw fit for it to happen the way it did to show his mighty miracle-working power.

Chapter 3 – ICU Days

I was in the ICU for weeks, and the ICU crew was excellent. During that time, I needed nourishment, so I had to have a feeding tube. The tube had an opening that entered my left side directly below my ribs. There was a specific time for feeding; a nurse would come in and open a can of nourishment, pour it in a syringe, and squeeze it in the opening of the tube, which kept me in a balance of nutrients although I had lost weight. That was the best way to keep me healthy.

Sanford and my Dad spent every single night in the ICU waiting room. Sanford would sometimes come in to see me, hold my hand, talk to me, and play music. My Mom and Dad would see me every day, as well. Other close family members would also come visit to see how I was doing and show continuous support. Dr. Stofko would come in to check on me every day and keep Sanford and my parents up to date on my progress. He didn't know how much damage the aneurysm had caused to my left side. He said that I possibly couldn't walk or move my left arm and hand.

After being in ICU for about two weeks, Dr. Stofko started to take me off the ventilator about thirty minutes at a time, to the point that I didn't struggle; I was completely taken off. I woke up a little later and had no idea what happened. Sanford was right there. I remember touching my head, and I asked Sanford what happened to my hair, and he told me I had an aneurysm. The only thing I remember is a little voice saying, "Mommy, wake up."

At that time, Sanford didn't want to tell me that I had six other aneurysms in total to scare or upset me. Shortly after, I was given a tracheotomy, which is often needed to assist breathing during recovery.[2] I was in ICU for a few more weeks. While there, I developed close relationships with a head nurse, Larry. My family could depend on him to take special care of me, and he kept them notified of any updates.

As I progressed, Dr. Stofko spoke with Sanford and my parents about transitioning to a therapy-type hospital that could help with moving around more and getting some physical therapy I hadn't had much of. Although nurses came in to move my arms and legs when I was just lying in the bed to make sure I didn't get bed sores and blood clots. I started to progress daily, and the next phase was decided to change hospitals for continued improvement. I left my room from the ICU and was a little sad to leave the wonderful ICU floor crew. Larry came out to the ambulance to see me off and gave me the warmest hug. I was so thankful to have been taken such great care of by the ICU staff family, but that would not be the only time I would see them. Through the series of other surgeries, I had to continue going to St. Mary's for subsequent medical procedures.

---

[2] Tracheostomy: https://www.mayoclinic.org/tests-procedures/tracheostomy/about/pac-20384673

Chapter 4 – Transition to the Next Phase

I got the trach removed during my days at Tennova North Hospital, which I was very happy about because I decided to finally see Zane.

I didn't want him to see me with a trach. I thought that he would be afraid and confused. My Mom and Sanford could go back to work full-time when they needed to. My Aunt Connie and my Daddy came by every day and took turns to be with me. Someone was always there.

I was never left alone. I call them my village, and I can always depend on them to help or assist in any way possible. Such as times, when I would often get tired of eating hospital food, I could make a call to my special bestie, Renee' Harley, to bring anything I'd ask for on her lunch break and sit, talk, and eat with me when she was able to. A visit from anyone was always welcome. At times, some would come to pray with me and bring gifts, cards, and food. All those things would lift my spirit; my Pastor Reginald Strong and his wife D'nese would check on me every day. There were so many from my church, Community Evangelistic Church, to be there for me and my family as well, too many to name individually.

Granny and Granddaddy took turns with GiGi, my mother, who cared for Zane the entire time because Sanford was with me every day that he could be and stayed with me at Tennova. I was taking several medications for different reasons; one specific medication in particular is called beta blockers. I took it to regulate my heart rate and open up veins and arteries to improve blood flow. A side effect was hallucination. I did have a crazy dream that was a hallucination. My dream was I had been arrested. I told Sanford to call our attorney because I had been mistreated by the police; it seemed so incredibly real. At that time, I couldn't understand why no one believed me. I was very happy when Dr Stofko took me off of it. I still had a feeding tube. After that, I had to pass a swallow test in order to be able to eat. While in the hospital room, a screen was brought in to view what and if I could swallow. There was a small camera put down my throat, and a video of my throat showed up on the screen. I had to first swallow a tic tac. It was very hard to swallow because I had to keep the camera down and focus on swallowing at the same time. Once I got the hang of it and swallowed, I was given applesauce next to test, which sounded easy but was not. I passed the swallow test with success. The first meal I asked for was a Big Mac; I'm not sure why I wanted that. I'm assuming just the taste of the two all-beef patties, special sauce, lettuce, cheese, pickles, and onions on a sesame seed bun sounded so good, so I just wanted it. That was a huge mistake because it did not agree with my system at all. Even though it tasted great, it wasn't worth the stomach issue I had that entire night. Sanford was asking me to put my glasses on so I could see. I told him I couldn't because I had contact lenses in my left eye, and that would make my vision blurry. The contact had been there the entire time, which no one knew until I told them. No one could get it out, and I couldn't get it either. I had to be taken to an eye doctor by ambulance. As I lay on the gurney, I did not have flashbacks, but I was thinking how uncomfortable it was. I was taken inside the ophthalmologist's office on the gurney. They told the doctor why I was there. She had a contact solution. She opened my eye, poured a few drops into my eye, gently put her finger on my eye, slid the contact down, and pulled it out of my eye. She examined my eye and praised God, but there was no damage to my eye. The contact was in my eye for so many weeks. Praise God, it did not disintegrate in my eye, which could have caused serious damage. I was on the gurney the entire time; it was so uncomfortable, but it was worth it. I could finally put my glasses on to see much better without blurry contact lenses. I was in an ambulance back to the hospital. It was freezing outside. I was covered with several thick heating blankets. I was excited to return to my room, mainly to get off the uncomfortable gurney. I could finally see decently.

During my stay at Tennova North, some therapists who tried to help with physical therapy did all they could, but they did not specialize in physical therapy. They helped with as much as they could. And I couldn't move my arm as well as I needed to. I had to get more progressive physical therapy. If not, my shoulder was on the verge of being frozen, which could have caused no movement at all. Being that my head was very fragile and I had to be very careful because the bone on the right side of my head had not been put back in, there were other aneurysms that had to be attacked, six more to be exact, in order for me to do any physical therapy, I was fitted for a medical helmet, I had to wear it anytime I was to get out of my wheelchair. My time at Tennova North Hospital was complete. The next hospital/rehab facility was Patricia Neal Rehabilitation. During my time there, I started with an introduction to physical therapy. The first day I went into the therapy room to meet my therapist, Melissa, I looked around, and everyone, in my opinion, was worse off than I was, or so I thought. I looked at Sanford and said I'm leaving. Everyone is old here. I'm not this bad. I was in denial at the time. In all actuality, I was in a much worse condition than most of them. I had to face the fact that I needed therapy. I was just tired of hospitals. I was so ready to go home, but I had a long road ahead of me, and there was so much that I had to work on. While I was at Pat Neal, I had occupational therapy, which involved working on my left wrist and fingers. I learned techniques that helped me get better motion and fine motor skills with my fingers, working on how to grip, not being able to do the smallest things like picking up a cup, which the therapist taught me how to relearn to put my clothes on, even though there were times I just wanted help, but I was to do things myself even if I got; or if something was too hard for me, I would definitely get help. Relearning how to do something that some would think is so easy, like putting a shirt on, learning how to do it the easiest way when the hand, wrist, and fingers are weak and do not move and work like they used to. On a particular Saturday session, the therapist rubbed a pen down my shin and asked me if I could feel it. I was shocked and brokenhearted when I had to tell him no. I couldn't feel it. He said that was ok, that's why you're here. I had to learn how to maneuver a wheelchair while in therapy as well. Doctors' orders were that the therapist had to watch my pulse because I was weak and critical to keep my blood pressure normal so that the other six aneurysms would stay stable and not be affected. It was very necessary that I did not exert myself. I also had speech therapy because my voice was not as strong as it used to be because of the trach I had for so many weeks. It somewhat damaged my voice. As of now, my voice sounds like I have a "frog" in my throat at times. There's an area in the front of my neck, in the throat area, that looks sunken in. I call it one of my beauty marks. That's a visual area. I used to share a portion of my journey with someone in a store. My beauty marks are there so I can tell God's goodness, grace, and mercy. My purpose is to share my journey with anyone who asks to minister to them. There was a point at a certain time when I questioned God. Why me? But honestly, why not me? It's taken a while to actually get to that point of my journey where God allows things to happen to display His miracle and handiwork. All for anyone to believe and see, and all of what He's capable of doing in my life or anyone he chooses to use.

When I look back on how it was touch and go, I could have gone on to be with Jesus. But He chose to save my life to allow me to stay on this earth to be a vessel for Him. I met some amazing therapists there, but after being there for three weeks, it was time to move on to a health and rehabilitation facility. At Beverly Park Place, I had therapy every day. During my time there, I started walking a little more with the help of Kathy, and I quickly bonded with her. She was not just my PT but a special friend. I started walking with a hemi-walker, along with an AFO (Ankle-foot orthoses), a medical brace used to be put around my ankle and placed in my shoe. It stabilizes my ankle so that it won't turn as I learn how to move my feet correctly, and it would help my stride as I relearn to walk.

While I was at Beverly Park Place, I was able to be picked up for an outing. Sanford would come to get me, and I would go home to hang out with him and the boys, but I had to be back at the facility by 9 p.m. And anytime anyone came to visit me there, they had to leave at 9, and no one could stay the night. I was so used to Sanford being with me and not leaving when I was at the hospital. I felt so alone and depressed there, but when my time was up and I could go home, it was a milestone.

I had been away from home since 2016. On my first night home, I had to adjust to moving around my house in a new wheelchair. We were blessed that our apartment complex allowed us to move to a lower-level apartment, which made it very easy to get around. Previously, we lived in a two-story apartment. I was extremely happy to be back home. It was an adjustment but a little piece of heaven to be with my family. I could see Zane every day and Tyson more. I really missed them so much. I wanted to get back in the swing into "Mommy mode," but I still had to take it easy because I still had six other aneurysms that had to remain stable until time to take care of them at certain times. I was very careful and kept my helmet on when standing or moving around. I started outpatient therapy there once a week for an hour. I had a great physical therapist there. Kathy was such a great therapist, friend, and prayer partner who showed me exactly what to do when getting out of my wheelchair using an AFO. I used this in my shoe, which helped me learn how to re-walk and keep my ankle straight. Even though it was not the most comfortable, it really helped me go through the original motion of walking. I missed walking. That said, always be grateful and appreciate being able to move and go along with your daily duties. In the blink of an eye, it was taken away from me instantly from the effects of the aneurysm. I will never take how God continues to bless and heal me for granted. While in therapy, I had blood work done often to ensure my hemoglobin and platelet levels were as normal as possible. If the levels were not high enough, I had to be admitted to the hospital for an overnight stay to get a blood transfusion to raise my levels. The process normally takes a couple of hours. My blood type is rare, with so many different antibodies, the hospital would request the type of blood from the blood bank, and once admitted, the nurse would come and start an IV in my hand to use for the transfusion.

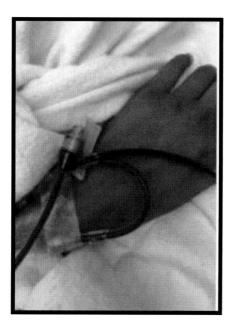

Picture taken during a transfusion

I'm so used to being poked; it doesn't hurt unless a nurse can't find a good vein, or it would roll. I normally advise them on the arm and where to stick once the blood came, depending on how low my blood level would determine how many units I had to receive. I normally would get at least two units. It would take up to several hours to drop. After the last unit, they would check my levels to see if units helped raise. I never had to be there alone. Sanford was there throughout the admission process until I was discharged the next day. After home for a couple of months and adjusting to life at home, I had other checkups with Dr. Stofko, as well as CT scans. After consultations with Dr. Stofko, it was time to have my bone/skull placed back on my head.

Selfie taken right after the bone/skull replacement.

This procedure was again another process that took several months, as it was when it was removed. I couldn't sleep the night before I went to the hospital. I stayed up and prayed all night until I fell asleep. It was the most terrified I have been thus far. I wasn't sure of what to expect. I arrived at the hospital at 5 a.m. and checked in for surgery by 7. It would take about an hour to get prepped for surgery, IV, blood work, and anything else I needed, then the waiting game for the doctor to finish any prior surgeries he had to complete, depending on how long they were.

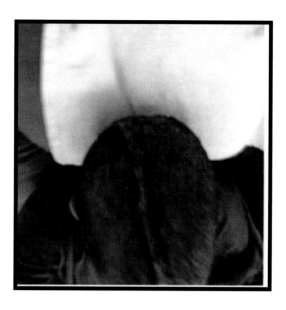

Picture taken after replaced bone healed and the first haircut to start over.

Chapter 5 – The Other Six Aneurysms

Going into 2018, Doctor Stofko wanted to coil the additional aneurysms. In January, Dr. Stofko performed coiling to block blood flow into the aneurysm, which weakened the area in the wall of an artery. In coiling, a catheter is passed through the groin up into the artery containing the aneurysm, and then platinum coils are released. The coils cover the inside portion of the aneurysm; this allows the aneurysm to stay completely stable and does not grow larger, and it will not burst. This process was done throughout before the last aneurysm was coiled.

I met with Dr. Stofko, and he showed me the last image of the CT scan that was done. It showed a grey shadow over the right side of my skull; he explained that it was the fluid buildup, he explained the plan to remove it, and followed by telling me he had decided to leave St. Mary's Hospital. He had been with me and worked on every procedure that I had. I was so sad; however, he had discussed my health and every detail of my medical case with another Neurosurgeon whom he completely trusted with my case, Dr. Chitale, who is at Vanderbilt Hospital in Nashville. I was certain that I was in the best care, but there was none like Dr. Stofko and the entire Neuro staff. The Lord gave me the best of the best. His plan was perfect because Dr. Stofko was working that particular Christmas when everything happened. He knew exactly how to treat the rupture and what to do over the period of time to handle the others as well.

Chapter 6 – The Last Aneurysm

Dr. Stofko wanted to make sure all the fluid buildup was removed as soon as possible. Draining the fluid was called a bedside procedure. I didn't have to go to an operating room and was not put to sleep. Dr. Stofko and one of his nurse practitioners were there. He placed a surgical cloth on the top near the right side of my head where the bone was placed so he could get right on top of the fluid, gave medication to relax and numb my head, and then cut a small incision. A small tube was pushed gently into where the opening of the small incision was. The tube had a ball on the end of the tube; the fluid started draining into the tube. I was there overnight to make sure all the fluid that resembled blood was completely drained. The following day, I had an MRI that showed the area was clear. The fluid was all drained successfully.

Dr. Stofko removed the tube with no problem, and that day, I was released; I was so happy to be going home. However, there was time to schedule my last aneurysm to be clipped. The time had come for the procedure. I prepped myself and went to the doctor to have my blood levels checked to make sure I didn't need a blood transfusion. When I got the results of my blood count, they were sent over to Dr. Stofko's office to show that I was ready for the surgery. There was a time when my blood count was low before surgery, and I had to get a blood transfusion before I was able to have the surgery. What normally would happen was I would be admitted into the hospital a day before and get a couple of units of blood. Once I had enough to raise my hemoglobin levels, I was set to have surgery.

Chapter 7 – Home Sweet Home

While at home, I had to start to relearn how to tie my shoes as well as zip up my coat and button-up shirts, which may seem like something small, but they were big milestones to me.

When my Pastor, Pastor Strong, gave examples of things in a sermon, like he had to relearn to button his shirt and lift his leg to put his pants on, I knew exactly how he felt. Sometimes, I would feel so helpless, BUT GOD! However, before relearning how to do anything, Sanford was there as my husband and helpmate, helping me with things that I couldn't do on my own yet. He helped me get to the bathroom, help me with a shower, and put on my clothes.

In Feb 2018, I had two back-to-back surgeries that completed the last aneurysm. Aneurysms are complete. I would only be seen for follow-ups for CT scans and MRA since Dr. Stofko moved to Charleston, South Carolina. I would start going to Vanderbilt Hospital in Nashville to see Dr. Chitale. After this last surgery, I was able to shop and plan for Zane's 6th birthday. He loved The Wizard of OZ as I did as well. We purchased Broadway play tickets, surprised him with Tennessee Theatre, and went as a family, which was extra special because I missed his 5th birthday. I was not allowed to be released from Beverly Park Place, so I missed his party.

Zane at his 5th Birthday Party

I planned what I could. Sanford, family, and friends set up and did everything as long as Zane was ok; I was fine but sad. I saw my baby boy afterward, with pictures, cake, and balloons. God made it alright. I felt the Lord healing my heart at particular times when I felt sad, and me and God. There have been certain times when no one would understand, and it was just Him and me. One time specifically, I couldn't see the eclipse. It was just me and the (Son). Everyone told me how great it was, but I was left out, and that was ok. I was thankful to be here, still alive and well, and even to this day, when times are rough, I pray and continue to just say thank you, Lord. I chose to remember that life is so extremely special. I could have slipped away in my sleep or died when I fell on the steps at my house when the accident happened.

Chapter 8 – Always Family

Being home and knowing I was done with surgery felt so wonderful. I was happy to be able to get out and be with family and friends. It wasn't always easy getting out. Thank God we had an SUV because I always had to have a wheelchair with me because I wasn't walking well at all. We had to lug it around everywhere we went, and whoever, family or friend, would make sure I had it. Sanford and I were always an on-the-go type of family. He always made sure if it was somewhere we were invited to or liked to go, we went to church, mall, family dinners, etc.

First family outing to celebrate September birthdays

The first Mother's Day after aneurysm

Delta Mardi Gras Ball, Emerald Foundation Event, family dinners, cookouts, and it always felt good to get out and be with the ones who love and support me. I might be slow, but I did not let anything stop me. As long as I was able to go, I went. I thanked God for the drive to go. Praise God that I did not have depression or suffer from PTSD. I was blessed to see Zane graduate from preschool in May 2017 at God's Creative Enrichment Center. I missed most of the time he was there, but I was home just in time to see my little sweet face graduate. His first big boy milestone was that my hair was still growing back from being cut. I had special family and friends who would meet me wherever I was going and wrap my scarf around my head because my hair had not completely grown back yet. I might have missed

Zane's preschool days, but he was right at home to shop and prepare for his first day of Kindergarten at Emerald Academy.

What's so special is my family also planned a crab boil dinner with all my immediate family. They knew that seafood was my favorite food and kept the Christmas tree up for me, and we exchanged gifts like it was Christmas day all over again until April 25, 2017. It was so special to be around them and celebrate being home. Since being home, we had to find a way to get back to some sort of normal schedule. My family was always there to help make it normal for Sanford and me. We devised a schedule that worked for a while until I was able to be at home by myself. Sanford had to get back to work full-time. The schedule went as such: my Mom came over in the morning before she went to work; she brought over or prepared breakfast and got my medicine ready. Sanford would take Zane to school. Mom would leave for work as Aunt Connie came to sit with me, fixed lunch, helped me with therapy, and walked with me outside around the apartment complex so that I would get my walking in every day. Aunt Connie stretched my legs out to loosen me up before walking and did arm exercises as well. Sanford continued to walk with me at home after work. He also continued to coach flag football, which I enjoyed going to practice and the games with Zane. On game day, my family was right there to support and help me to get situated with my wheelchair behind the sidelines so that Sanford could tend to coach duties. It was fun last year for Falcon flag football. Before I started therapy at Drayer Physical Therapy in Karns, where I started walking with a walker, doing a little more with a different maneuver to strengthen my left leg, hip, and foot, where it was a drop foot, I researched a device called Bioness L300; it was very expensive, and after meeting with a company representative on how it worked and learning more about the product and actually using it, I knew that would benefit and help me walk.

When I put it on, it sent stimulation to my foot and lifted up so I could step without my foot dragging or turning. It kept it straight. I knew if I could get this, I would use it every day. The only problem was my insurance wouldn't cover it. How was I going to afford it? Lord, help me, as you have already brought me this far. So, we brainstormed, let's raise the money! We decided to have a raffle and raffled off a 55-inch, 4K smart TV; tickets were $10. Family, friends, and church members bought and sold tickets. By the time the raffle date ended and was complete, everyone turned in the money to me and Sanford. We raised the total amount needed to purchase the device Bionness L300. It was delivered to my house. I was trained on how it worked. I wore it every day and took it to therapy at Drayer Physical Therapy. Praise God, so many people supported my efforts to purchase this device for my foot. Otherwise, I would more than likely drag my left foot walking without it. My family and friends have always been there for me. My first birthday, when I was able to come home, was nice just being able to go out to eat, no matter what I looked like. I didn't mind showing my bald head; I was happy to be home and be with my family.

36th Birthday dinner at Wasabi

Chapter 9 – "Made A Way"- My Journey Song

My parents took me to my first follow-up Neuro appointment at Vanderbilt Hospital in June 2019. Dr. Chitale performed a routine surgical exam and saw that everything was stable. In recovery, he told me everything was fine. My report was given to me, and it stated **100% occlusion of ancurysms. Look at God!!** *He Made A Way!!* I was taken off of the blood thinner (Clopidogrel) that I was on and just asked to take aspirin and stay on a few other medications that I was already taking. Furthermore, they recommended that I continue to see my hematologist as always.

Dr Chitale said he would see me next year. I'm still continuing therapy when I can, always out and about with family and friends. I love seeing and being around my son, Zane, who is why I continue to strive and do my best to regain more strength in my left leg and hip. I may not ever be the same with walking or running before the aneurysm, but I was certainly doing better.

When I was in dire need of the Bionness L300 and short on funds, I never knew how God would make a way. I had decided to ask a very close family church friend to borrow the funds to purchase this new device and pay them back over time; their words were, don't worry about it. This is God's money, and they are blessed. Me with the Bioness L300 Go. I thank the Lord for blessing me with the new device for my foot. I just cried and praised God because, again,

"He Made A Way!"

It hasn't been easy relearning everything over again. At one point, I was running after my 4-year-old, working a full-time job, and everything a wife and mommy do to having a ruptured brain aneurysm and not knowing if I would even live life. The Lord has always been right on there. In so many instances, I couldn't work and lost my job, but God has always sent someone to bless me. When I didn't know where funds would come from to help pay bills in my household. My disability was deposited into my account almost out of nowhere, and I had no idea when it would happen, but yes, as you should already know, *"He Made A Way!"*

As for the present day, I'm continuing to do the best I can to share my story with anyone on social media. As much as I dislike speaking to large crowds. I've given my testimony and will continue to do so. I've come to realize I was made for this journey. Some decided not to continue to run this journey with me. Sanford had served his purpose in my life for many years, and I thank God for the husband and caregiver he was. God placed us together for a specific reason. Although we decided to part ways, we continue to raise our sons together and remain friends. But as life goes on, there may be some that won't continue on this journey with me, but my Lord and Savior has never left my side, from the time on Christmas Day 2016 passed out and unconscious on the steps at my apartment, to the operating table bleeding on the brain, to operating on seven aneurysms, to wearing an uncomfortable helmet to protect my head, to replace the bone/skull, to the many days of physical therapy, to the many days of doctor appointments for a checkup, to feeling alone and not being able to see my sons for weeks, to finally going home, send being able to get to my new normal of life, and be with my family and friends, I've met so many and been touched by so much love from some I knew and some I didn't know, Blessings from near and far.

God revealed Himself in ways I didn't even realize at the time. As I was in the ICU while my family was in the ICU waiting room, they met and prayed with people of families who were in the ICU as well. They were a blessing and being blessed as well. God orchestrated my journey so beautifully that I thought about other times and places when I could have had the aneurysm. I could have been by myself, alone driving, out of town, with no hospital nearby, and many places when I could not have made it. God knew how it would be best for me, even though some may not understand why it had to happen. I've heard some say, *"You're too young to have something like that happen to you."* There was a time when I would question God. However, some nights, when I felt lonely or felt like no one really understood, the Holy Spirit would soothe my heart through a phone call or even a text of encouragement to lift my spirits. I've come to realize I was made for this journey. God ordered this ruptured aneurysm to save souls and show a miracle through handiwork. I was not built to break. There are probably many things that God would have me do. But I'm extremely blessed to be a mother. Zane found me when I had my aneurysm. I'm blessed to have made wonderful memories with Zane. Zane is now attending Berean Christian School, where he had a Bible Lesson 7 Test. He responded with this. "It truly touched my heart because I'm witnessing how the Lord is working in his life."

Me and Zane

Christmas Shoot 2019 – Zane's third-grade test at Berean Christian School

Chapter 10 – My Village

The journey continues with the help of my Lord and Savior and my Village, whom I love to no end. God knew exactly the kind of dedicated family and loyal friends that I needed in my life. They have blessed me in unexplainable ways. There are so many others to list by name or picture individually. However, their love has inspired me to share the way God's miracle-working power. I may not move and walk as quickly as I used to, but my village is always so willing to wait on me and be right by my side or push me in my wheelchair if needed for long-distance walking.

As for the present day, I'm continuing to do the best I can to share my story with anyone on social media. As much as I dislike speaking to large crowds, I've given my testimony and will continue to do so. I've come to realize I was made for this journey. Some decided not to continue to run this journey with me. Sanford had served his purpose in my life for many years, and I thank God for the husband and caregiver he was. God placed us together for a specific reason. Although we decided to part ways, we continue to raise our sons together and remain friends. But as life goes on, there may be some who won't continue on this journey with me. However, my Lord and Savior has never left my side: from the time on Christmas Day 2016 when I passed out and was unconscious on the steps at my apartment, to the operating table bleeding on the brain, to operating on seven aneurysms, to wearing an uncomfortable helmet to protect my head, to replace the bone/skull, to the many days of physical therapy, to the many days of doctor appointments for checkups, to feeling and not being able to see my sons for weeks, to finally going home, and being able to get to my new normal of life and be with my family and friends, I've met so many and been touched by so much love from some I knew and some I didn't know. Blessings from near and far.

LaShaya Porter Miller

36

I've had seven aneurysms. As seven is the number of completions, it is finished for now. I praise and thank God. He allowed me to survive a ruptured brain aneurysm so that I could share my journey with the world from the time I was diagnosed with sickle cell anemia at six months old to the age of 35 with a ruptured brain aneurysm. I'm continually amazed at the goodness of God. If you don't know Jesus, just know that my life shows that he's so real and continues to work miracles because I'm here living my life.

It hasn't been easy, but I know I'm a living witness and have brought people to know Jesus and grow closer to Him.

About the Author

LaShaya, better known as Shay, is a Christian, a great Mom, a sister, an aunt, a niece, and a remarkable daughter. Shay holds family and friends close to her heart and loves them immensely. Her desire is that everyone who reads this book will feel encouraged and blessed and understand that they, too, can be overcomers, just as she is an overcomer. Shay has pushed through so much adversity; however, she maintained her kind and caring nature, gentle spirit, and loving heart. Be blessed.

Made in the USA
Monee, IL
21 November 2024

70842554R00029